Grimm's Fairy Tales

ANNO'S TWICE TOLD TALES
The Fisherman and His Wife & The Four Clever Brothers

by The Brothers Grimm & Mr. Fox
illustrated by **Mitsumasa Anno**

Philomel Books

There was once a fisherman and his wife. They lived together in a poor little hut close to the sea. Every day the fisherman went out in his boat and fished and fished and fished. However, there were not many fish left in the sea, and so he didn't have much luck. But suddenly one day as he was sitting in his boat fishing, the hook went down, deep down, and when he pulled it up, there he had a big golden fish. And the fish said to him:

One day, at the edge of the forest, little Freddy Fox found a book. Someone must have forgotten it, or dropped it, he thought. Freddy hurried home to show the book to his father. It seemed to have two stories in it. "Oh, please, will you read this book to me?" he asked. Mr. Fox was rather sleepy, but finally he agreed. But then he said something funny: "I'll only read one story at at time, and I'll read each story only once." Why did he say that? Freddy wondered. Mr. Fox opened the book.

"Listen, fisherman, I beg you to let me live. I am not a real fish; I am an enchanted prince. How would it help you if you killed me? I wouldn't taste good to you, anyway. Put me back into the water and I'll give you a wish."

"Well, now," said the fisherman, "you needn't make a fuss about it. A fish that can talk—I would surely have let you go, anyway." With that, he put him back into the clear water, and the fish disappeared. And the fisherman went home to his wife.

Hmm…this book is full of gibberish — you know, hard words. See, that great big place is the ocean. There's a boat in it, and a fisherman in the boat. A fisherman is someone who makes a living catching fish, sort of like a hunter, someone who catches animals. Now, Freddy, never forget this: Foxes are what hunters want most of all. If you're not careful, you could get caught and end up as a furpiece around some lady's neck.

"Husband," scolded his wife, Isabel, "haven't you caught anything today?"

"Well," said the fisherman, "I caught a golden fish who said he was an enchanted prince, so I let him go again."

"But didn't you wish yourself something?" asked his wife.

"No," said the fisherman. "What could I have wished for?"

"Oh!" exclaimed his wife. "Here we live in this poor little hut. You could have wished us a pretty little house. He would give us that, surely."

Oh, good. I recognize this now. This is like that story a Japanese fox once told me. It goes: Once upon a time there was an old fisherman. His name was—let me see now—oh, I forget. Anyway the old man went down to the sea, and on the way he ran into some children who were teasing a turtle. You remember that turtle, don't you, Freddy? There was a story about a turtle and a rabbit in another book I read you. In this story, though, the old fisherman scolds the children for teasing the turtle.

"Oh," said the fisherman. "Why should he do that for me?"

"Well," said his wife, "after all, you caught him and let him go again, didn't you? I'm sure he will do this for you in return. Now go right down there and ask him!"

It's funny, Freddy, the fisherman himself, mind you, catches fish all the time, and eats them, too. Yet he gets mad at the children for teasing a turtle. Fishermen are hard to figure out. Anyway, the old man set the turtle loose in the sea, and it swam away very happily. Then, the story goes, he went home and told his wife about it. But she got mad at *him* and said, "You might have caught us some fish for our dinner while you were at it! Why are you so good to a turtle, anyway? What did a turtle ever do for us?"

The fisherman didn't really want to do it, but he did not want to go against his wife's wishes, either, and so he went off to the seaside. As he came there, the sea was all gray and yellow and not at all so clear anymore. But he went and bent down and called out:
"Mannie, Mannie, Tempie, Tee,
Fishie, Fishie in the sea,
Isabel, my willful wife,
Wants a better way of life."

After that scolding, what could he do but go back down to the sea and try to catch a fish for dinner? There he was with his line out when who should appear but the turtle. At least, I think it was a turtle. It's a bit hard to tell from the picture, but—yes, that's definitely a turtle. It's in the water so only its head shows. This book must have been done by a pretty good artist, because you can tell from just its head that that's a turtle. Right, Freddy?

Soon the fish came swimming along and said, "Well, what does she want, then?"

"Oh," said the fisherman. "After all, I caught you and let you go. Now my wife says I should really have wished myself something when you offered it. She doesn't want to live in our poor little hut anymore. She would dearly like to have a pretty little house."

"Go home, then," said the fish. "She has that now."

"Thank you for saving my life," said the turtle. "Now I have an invitation from our princess. She would like to invite you to the sea king's castle. She wants to thank you personally. So, now, if you would just get on my back, please." Now, Freddy, if anyone you don't know says something like that to you, don't you ever go off with him, do you hear? The sea king's castle is at the bottom of the sea. A fox or a person who went down there would probably drown.

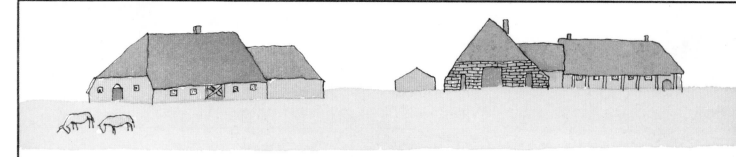

So the fisherman went home and his wife wasn't sitting in the poor little hut anymore, but there stood a pretty little house, and she was sitting in front of it on a bench. She took his hand and said to him:

"Just come in and look at it. See, now, isn't this better?"

So they went in, and in the house was a little hall and a parlor and a kitchen and a dining room; upstairs was a sleeping room in which stood their bed. In back of the house was a little yard with chickens and ducks, and a garden with vegetables and fruit trees growing in it.

"See," said Isabel, "isn't that nice?"

"Yes," said the fisherman, "and so let it be. Now we can live contentedly."

"Well, we'll think about that," said his wife.

With that they had a bite to eat and went to bed.

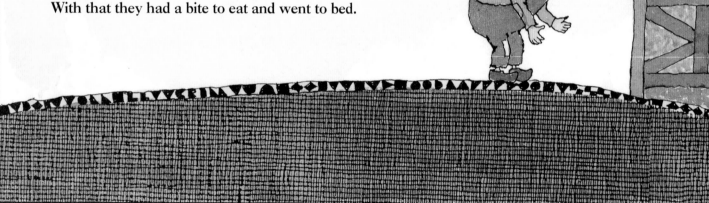

Well, this put the old man on the spot. He knew that the sea king's castle was at the bottom of the sea. And, while he certainly wanted to go there and meet the princess, he was afraid. It was true that he had saved the turtle, but it was also true that he had caught an awful lot of fish in his day. He couldn't help but wonder if this invitation wasn't a trick for the purpose of getting even with him.

So all went well for a week or two, but then Isabel said to her husband:

"Listen, man, this house is much too small, and the yard and garden are so tiny. The fish might really have given us a bigger house. I want to live in a stone mansion. Go to the fish and tell him to give us a mansion."

"No, wife," said the fisherman. "The fish has already given us a nice house. I don't want to go bothering him again. It might displease him."

"Go!" said his wife. "He can do that perfectly well and gladly. Ask him."

You would have thought, then, that the old man would pass up the offer. But he couldn't help thinking that if the princess were very beautiful, it might be worth going to see her even if he did drown. He just couldn't make up his mind what to do. So he told the turtle he would let him know later. In this picture you can see he went around to his neighbors to ask them for their advice.

When he came to the sea, the water was all purple and gray and thick, but it was still quiet. So he went and bent down and called:

> "Mannie, Mannie, Tempie, Tee,
> Fishie, Fishie in the sea,
> Isabel, my willful wife,
> Wants a better way of life."

"Well, what does she want, then?" asked the fish.

"Oh," said the fisherman. "She wants to live in a big stone mansion."

"Go home, then," said the fish. "She has it now. She is sitting in the front garden, enjoying a feast."

After talking it over with a number of people, the fisherman decided that he would invite the turtle and the princess to visit him, instead. Human beings, you know, Freddy, are pretty wily. It doesn't say so, but his idea was to find out what the turtle was really planning. If the princess would agree to come up on land, then it probably would be safe for a landlubber like him to go down to visit the sea king.

"Didn't he also want to see if he could find out first just how pretty the princess really was?" you ask. Freddy, that's good thinking! You've really got a point. Maybe he really was thinking about that. Well, anyway, the old man went back to the sea and called out, "Turtle, oh, Turtle. I want to invite the princess to come to my village, instead. Won't you please bring her up here?"

So the fisherman left and thought he would go home, but when he reached it, just as the fish had said, there was a big stone mansion, and his wife was seated in front of it at a table laden with food.

"Come and have some dinner," she said. When they had eaten, she took him by the hand and said, "Now come inside." Together they walked from room to room. "See?" said Isabel. "Isn't it beautiful?"

"Oh, yes," agreed the fisherman. "And so let it be. Now we will live in this fine stone mansion forever and be well satisfied."

"Well, we'll think that over and sleep on it," said Isabel. And with that they went to bed.

When the mayor of the village heard about all this, he went to see the fisherman. "Well, well," he said to the old man, "I hear you have invited the sea princess to our village. How about coming to my place tonight for dinner?" I think he probably had meant this to be a sort of trial run for the princess's reception. But, of course, it wouldn't have done at all. I mean, you can't have a cooked fish sitting on the table like that when you are entertaining the princess from the sea kingdom!

Anyhow, when the fisherman showed up for dinner, the mayor had some more news for him. "I told the lord governor about this," said the mayor, "and he was very enthusiastic about it. He said to me: 'Invite the sea princess over here, to my mansion. We'll have a wonderful party for her. This is a great honor, so see that everything is done right. Spare no expense. I'll take care of everything.' But we can talk about all this over dinner," said the mayor. "And do let me give you a cup of sake with your meal."

The next morning Isabel woke up early and jumped out of bed. The fisherman was still sleeping, but she poked him with her broomstick.

"Man, get up!" she said. "Just look out of the window. See? Why couldn't you become king and rule over all that land out there?"

"Oh, dear wife," said the fisherman. "I don't want to be king."

"Well," said his wife, "if *you* don't want to be king, *I* do! Go to that fish and tell him that!"

"Oh, no, wife!" protested the fisherman. "I don't want to tell him that!"

"Why on earth not?" said Isabel. "Go right down there. I *must* be king!"

The old fisherman was very fond of sake, and he let the mayor fill up his cup again and again. He had never drunk so much in his life and before he knew it he was quite tipsy. He sang and he danced and he boasted. "Yes, sir," he said, "I'll be glad to bring the princess to the lord governor's mansion. And while I'm at it I could bring fifty or so ladies-in-waiting! How would that be?"

At the end of the evening, the old fisherman fell sound asleep; the mayor put him to bed in the guest room for the night. Secretly, the mayor was beginning to hope that the lord governor would give him a medal or something for getting the princess to his mansion. So the next day, the mayor poked the old man and said, "Hey, Grandpa, wake up! Go get that turtle to fix things up with the sea princess!"

The fisherman was very upset. "This is not right," he thought, but he went anyway. And as he came to the sea, it was all dark and gray and the waves were rough. He went and bent down and called:

"Mannie, Mannie, Tempie, Tee,
Fishie, Fishie in the sea,
Isabel, my willful wife,
Wants a better way of life."

"Well, now what does she want?" asked the fish.
"Oh!" said the fisherman. "She wants to be king."
"Go home, then," said the fish. "She is the king."

The old man rubbed the sleep out of his eyes and set off. There wasn't a puff of wind, so none of the other fishermen were going out to sea. But the old man went down to the water's edge. He could hardly believe he had gotten so carried away the night before that he had actually promised to bring the princess to the lord governor's mansion by himself! What a terrible fix he was in now!

He called out, "Turtle, oh, Turtle, come and hear my plea!" The turtle appeared right away. "This is a request from the mayor and the lord governor, not just from me. It would make all of us very happy if the princess would come to the lord governor's mansion for a party in her honor. Nobody has to thank me. But, please, just get her and some of her people to come," the old man begged.

So the fisherman returned and found that the mansion had become a big castle with a wonderful high tower. A sentry stood beside the door, and there were many soldiers with drums and trumpets! As he came inside the castle, he found his wife sitting on a high throne. She had a crown of pure gold on her head and a scepter in her hand. He called up to her:

"Oh, wife, are you now king of the land?"

"Yes," said his wife. "Now I am king."

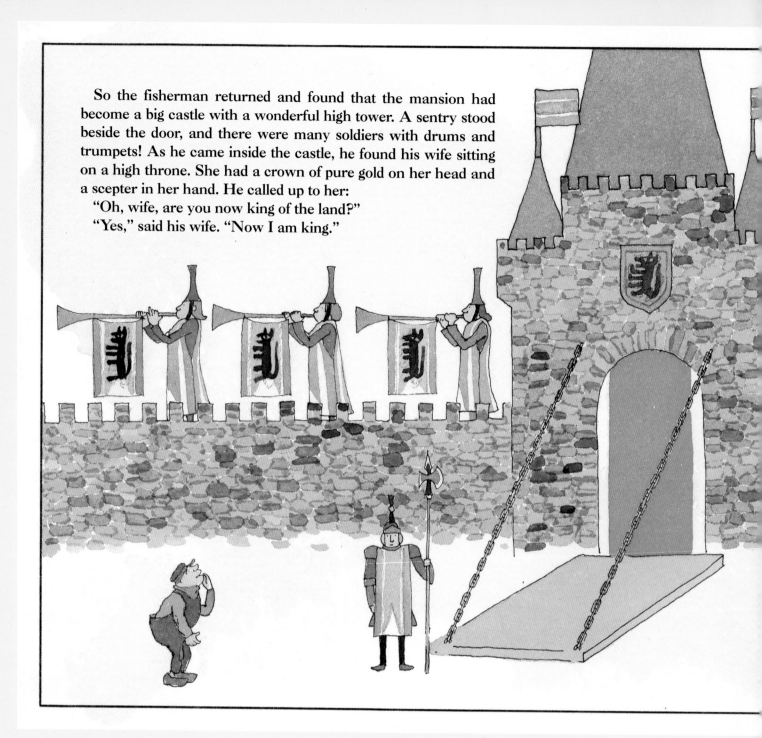

Evidently the turtle didn't give a clear answer one way or the other to this request, so the old man went home—only to be summoned, this time, by the lord governor. The lord governor had had all of the fishermen in the country catching fish every day and then throwing them back in the sea. Naturally, the fishermen didn't like this. By this time there was quite a commotion about it. Trembling, the old man went to the lord governor's mansion. Would he be blamed for this trouble?

"Oh, wife, how nice it is that you are king!" he said. "Now we have nothing more to wish for."

"No, man, that isn't true," said his wife, who looked very restless. "There isn't enough for me to do here. The time goes so slowly—I can't stand it anymore. You must go to the fish again. It's not enough being king. I want to be emperor!"

"Oh, no, wife!" said the fisherman. "I don't want to tell that to the fish!"

"What!" said his wife. "I am the king and I tell you, you *must* go talk to the fish right away. I want to be emperor! Go tell him this minute!"

So he had to go, but he was really frightened. And as he went along, he thought to himself, "This just doesn't seem right. Emperor is too much to ask for—the fish will get tired of us in the end."

But to his surprise, the lord governor was in a wonderful mood. "I hear you've been invited to visit the princess in the sea king's castle," he said. "The mayor told me about it, and I had suggested you invite her to come here to my mansion, instead. But when I told the king about it, he said, 'Invite her to my palace, instead! We'll have a wonderful party for her. This is a great honor. Spare no expense. I'll pay for everything.' Now I'm counting on you, old man, to carry this out," the lord governor said to the fisherman.

When he came to the seaside, a wild wind was blowing. But he tied himself to a tree so he wouldn't be blown away, and he went and bent over and called:

"Mannie, Mannie, Tempie, Tee,
Fishie, Fishie in the sea,
Isabel, my willful wife,
Wants a better way of life."

"Well, now what does she want?" asked the fish.

"Oh, fish. She wants to be emperor," said the fisherman.

"Go home, then," said the fish. "She is emperor now."

So the old fisherman had to go down to the sea again. This time, there was a storm. The wind was terrible, almost strong enough to blow the old man away, and the water rose up in giant waves. No sensible fisherman would go near the sea at a time like this. But he had to go. He was afraid of the stormy sea, but he was even more afraid of the lord governor. In a feeble voice, he called out:

"Turtle, oh, Turtle, come and hear my plea! This is a request from the king himself, not just from me. The king would be very pleased if the princess would come to a party in his palace. He wants to give a ball in her honor. I don't need any thanks for myself, but please, won't you bring the princess and some of her people to my village? If you don't, I'll be in terrible trouble!"

So the fisherman went, and when he came to the castle, he found it all made of polished marble, with alabaster statues and golden decorations. And inside, there sat his wife on a throne. She wore a huge golden crown and held in one hand the imperial globe. The fisherman called out:

"Wife, are you now emperor?"

"Yes," she replied. "I am emperor."

"Oh, wife," he said, "how happy I am for you!"

"Husband!" she said. "Don't stand there like that! It isn't enough for me just to be emperor. I want to become the pope! Go back to the fish and tell him!"

Meantime, the king's palace was bustling with activity. Carpets were replaced and walls painted. New flowers were planted in the gardens. The orchestra began practicing waltzes. The cooks were busy preparing for the feast. The fish stores were all temporarily closed, and all of the cats and weasels in the land were sent off to rest in the zoo for a while. This was the biggest thing that had ever happened in the country!

"Oh, wife," said the fisherman, "what are you asking? You can't become a pope; surely the fish can't do that."

"Don't argue," said Isabel. "If he can make an emperor, he can make a pope as well. Go along, now, and tell him."

Then what should happen but a rumor got started! People saw all the preparations at the palace and said to each other: "A wedding! I hear that the king is going to take another wife, the princess from under the sea, the most beautiful woman in the whole world!" This had all the people in the kingdom worried. "Whatever is our king thinking of?" they said. "The sea king will be angry. We'll be lucky if we don't end up in a war!"

So he went back to the sea again, and
in despair and terror he kneeled and called:
   "Mannie, Mannie, Tempie, Tee,
   Fishie, Fishie in the sea,
   Isabel, my willful wife,
   Wants a better way of life."
"Well, now what does she want?" asked the fish.
"Oh," said the fisherman. "She wants to be the pope!"
"Go home, then," said the fish. "She is pope now."

The old man hurried down to the sea again. The turtle hadn't promised to bring the princess
to the party yet. The fisherman made up his mind to stay there until he got the turtle to help
him. The storm grew worse and worse. He tied himself to a tree to keep from being blown out
to sea. But it wasn't the sea he was afraid of—he was really afraid of going home to face the
angry people.

Then he heard a small voice through the roar of the wind. It was the turtle. He said, "Nobody from the sea king's realm is going to come up on land as long as that weird rumor is going around about your king marrying the sea princess. And furthermore, the sea isn't going to calm down until that rumor calms down, too." The old fisherman apologized over and over again, but the turtle had gone.

So he went, and when he came back to his home, it was like a big church with towers all around it. Inside, everything was lit up with hundreds of candles. His wife was richly dressed and sat upon a throne that was even higher than before.

"Wife," he said, looking at her carefully and respectfully, "are you really the pope now?"

"Yes," she said, "I am pope."

"Oh, wife," he said, "how nice that you are pope. How happy you must be!"

But the next morning, as the sun began to rise, Isabel leaned over one end of the bed and looked out of the window. And when she saw the sun coming up, "Ha!" she thought, "why can't I, too, make the sun come up—and the moon as well?"

"Husband," she said aloud, and poked him with her elbow. "Wake up now, and go see the fish. Tell him I want to be God."

The fisherman, when he heard this, jumped right out of bed.

"Oh, no, wife," he said, and fell before her on his knees. "That the fish can't do. I beg you, be satisfied with what you have now!"

At that, she became so angry she stamped her foot and screamed, "No, no, I can't stand it any longer! Tell the fish I want to be God. I want to make the sun and the moon rise. I am the pope and I order you to go tell him!"

Weeks and weeks went by, but the sea didn't calm down. One day a famous wise man went to see the king. "As long as this storm continues," the wise man said, "the gardens can't be tended and the preparations for the feast can't go on. The grapes are about to drop off the vines. The cows have stopped giving milk. You can see that the sea king is angry. He probably thinks, 'Who do those people think they are, trying to get the princess to come up on land? Maybe it's some kind of trick!'"

Finally, the mayor and the lord governor and the king began to understand what had happened. You see, this wasn't the first time that people had tried to lure princesses and others from the sea kingdom into becoming their queens and wives and then, once they got them on land, had not let them go home. On the advice of the wise man, everyone went off to church. A million candles were lit, and all the people prayed as hard as they could to be forgiven for what they had done in the past.

So the fisherman pulled on his trousers and ran out of the palace. But outside there was a storm, and it raged so that he could hardly stay on his feet. Houses and trees blew over and the mountains quaked. Big rocks broke off and rolled into the sea, and the water rose up into big waves as high as church towers. The fisherman could scarcely hear his own voice as he called out:

"Mannie, Mannie, Tempie, Tee,
Fishie, Fishie in the sea,
Isabel, my willful wife,
Wants a better way of life."

"Well, now what does she want?" asked the fish.

Now the old fisherman could hear the far-off sound of church bells ringing. And then it seemed to him that the storm had begun to let up a bit, but still he didn't dare leave. He kept on calling the turtle: "Turtle, oh, Turtle, please come and listen to me. This is my last request." Finally, the turtle appeared and asked, "Well, what is it now?" By this time the old man was practically in tears. "Is it true that the storm won't stop because the sea king is angry?" he asked the turtle. "Everyone in my country is crying and saying the wind will blow all the

"Oh," said the fisherman. "She wants to make the sun and moon rise. She wants to be God!"

"Go home, then," said the fish. "You'll find her just where she belongs."

grapes off the vines. Please tell the sea king that our king is not even thinking of marrying the princess, even though she is so beautiful. In fact, he's in church at this very minute, praying for the storm to end and promising that he is not going to make anyone come up on land against their will. Oh, please tell this to your sea king!" "Go back home now," said the turtle, and it disappeared.

And so he did. She was back in the poor little house by the sea.
And there they both are to this day.

The turtle never came back with the sea king's response, but the storm ended. And, as bad as the wind had been, not a single grape fell off the vines. The fisherman's hut didn't blow away, either. Everything was back to the way it had been. The old man's wife was just the same, too. "What!" she scolded. "You didn't catch any fish again today! What a good-for-nothing old man you are!"

"Oh, please read it again," little Freddy begged. "But I told you I'd only read it once," Mr. Fox said,
as he pretended to go to sleep. You know why he said that, don't you? But Freddy didn't really mind
about the story. You see, it was Mr. Fox's day off, and what Freddy really wanted was just to sit on his
father's lap and have his father hold him close and talk to him.

There was once a poor farmer who had four sons. They were all so bright and hardworking that he could not tell which was the cleverest, but he loved them all equally. And when they were old enough to fend for themselves, he said to them:

"It is time for you to go out into the world and seek your fortunes. I have nothing I can give you but my blessing. Try to make something of yourselves."

So the brothers set out, and when they came to a crossroad the eldest one said, "Here we must part. Each must go a separate way. We will meet here again in four years to the day. In the meantime, we will try our luck. Let us see which of us fares the best."

But the second story in the book looked very interesting. "Daddy, if you can't read me this story, I think I'll ask Mother to read it," said Freddy. "Oh, no! Don't do that," said Mr. Fox. "I'll read it to you, after all. Now let me see. There's something funny written here. Oh, it says again that I can only read it once. Well, that's all I was going to do. So all right, I promise."

Look here, Freddy. Four boys are setting off on a trip. They are going to a faraway land where they'll hear and see all kinds of new things. They'll get an education, for sure. That's the way people used to study in the olden times. Each boy will go in a different direction and will learn something different. But I bet their father is going to miss them a lot while they're gone.

Soon the first brother met a man who was sitting on a bridge, fishing.

"Where are you going?" the man asked.

"I'm looking for someone to teach me a trade, so I can make my fortune," replied the boy.

"If it's a fortune you are seeking, come with me," said the man, "and I will teach you how to be a thief like me."

"No, no," the boy protested. "That is not an honest trade; I don't want to end up on the gallows!"

"Don't be afraid," said the man. "I'll only teach you how to take things so cleverly that no one will ever know you have done it. What you do with your skill is none of my affair."

So the boy studied for four long years and learned all that the man had to teach him.

"Now go on your way, my boy," said his teacher, "and remember that anything you want is yours for the taking. But whether you use your skill for good or for evil is up to you. Goodbye, and good luck to you."

Now it says there was a man fishing on a bridge that one of the boys wanted to cross. The man was pretty awful. "Hey, you," he said. "This is my bridge. What do you mean trying to sneak across it like that?" The world can be a rough place, you know, Freddy. Not everyone is always polite. "Oh, please let me cross," the boy said, but the man wouldn't. Then he said something really bizarre.

"You can't cross this bridge," he said. "You'll have to get some rope and cross over on that, just like in the circus." In a circus, you know, Freddy, they do scary things that regular people can't usually do. "All right," said the boy, "but let me cross the bridge to fasten my rope to the other side." Then the man got angry and strung up his fishing line across the river. "Now let me see you cross over on this!" he said. And the boy did it!

The second brother did not know what he wanted to become, either. But on his path he met an astronomer, a wise man who knew the secrets of the stars. The astronomer said to him, "Come with me, young fellow, and I will teach you to be a stargazer like me."

After four years, when the boy had finished his training, the wise man gave him a wonderful telescope. "With this, my boy, you can see everything that goes on in the heavens and also on earth," said the kind old man. "Use it wisely."

Hey, now look! All this stuff is for training the eyes. Humans have no sense of smell to speak of, and they can't see far at all. So they use this strange-looking tube for training. At first they look at things close by, then they get so they can see farther and farther away. It's like you, Freddy. You start out learning to catch mice by practicing on grasshoppers. And this training really works. Humans get so they can see quite far away.

But that's not all. It also says that those stars in the sky look like bears and scorpions. I can see how there could be a swan in the sky, but a fish?. . .Oh, I get it! They're training themselves to see things that are invisible. They are clairvoyants from a group of circus performers. They blindfold themselves and then guess what somebody from the audience is holding. But it's not magic—it's a trick.

There are some of us animals in the circus, too. There is something called "trick riding," where a human does somersaults and jumps rope on the back of a horse, and jumps with the horse over fire. These are toy horses made of wood. People are practicing riding no-handed. They're going to show how they can shoot rabbits, birds and foxes from the backs of galloping horses. Did you ever see a circus like that, Freddy?

The third brother became an apprentice to a hunter, who taught him how to shoot very well. And at the end of four years, the hunter gave him a gun as his reward.

"This is no ordinary gun," said the hunter. "With this gun you can hit anything you shoot at. But be careful how you use it. Now goodbye and good luck!"

Oh, look. Here it says: "You must not do dangerous things like this." And, Freddy, you must never play circus. You might get hurt. You must be sure to keep away from humans, too. If you got caught, your mother would cry her eyes out. And if they made you a target for the sharpshooter in the circus, even if everybody applauded and acclaimed you as the Death-defying Fox Target, it would be nothing to be proud of.

The fourth brother met a tailor who promised to teach him to sew. The boy did not really want to learn this trade, because he hated the idea of having to sit hunched over some garment all day.

"But what I will teach you is much more than just the tailor's craft," promised the man. "It is the honorable art of creating something unique."

So the boy agreed to stay and learn the tailor's skills. At the end of four years, the man gave him a needle. The boy thought this a very small reward for all his hard work.

Ah-ha! Look at this. A fox got caught and had its fur taken. That's why I'm always telling you that you've got to watch out for human beings. Human beings don't have nice fur like foxes do, so they make things called "clothes" to put on. And sometimes they wear some animal's fur. Tailors make the clothes. This tailor, it says, is taking the customer's measurements and telling him, "My, my, it looks like we've put on a bit of weight!"

But the tailor said, "This is a very special needle. With it you can sew anything you want to—be it as soft and slippery as a raw egg or as hard as a rod of steel. I know you will find it useful." So the lad thanked him and set out to meet his brothers and find out how they had fared.

But this is no ordinary tailor. This one also makes iron armor. And look what else he can make. Those are fake clothes that he's making. Not that you can't wear them. They look just like real clothes, but they have all sorts of hidden pockets. There's a pocket to hide a rabbit in, and another for a pigeon. It's a magician's outfit, in fact. Hmm. We've gotten pretty far into the story. It definitely is a story about a circus.

The four brothers met at the crossroad as they had planned. They greeted each other and then returned to their father. "What a fair wind has brought you safely back to me!" he exclaimed. "Now tell me all your adventures."

When each had told his story, the father was amazed and asked them to show him the skills they had learned. "There is a bird's nest very high up in that tree," he said. "Tell me how many eggs are in it."

The stargazer peered through his telescope. "Five," he said.

The father said to the next son, "Go and get them for me without disturbing the bird." The boy who had studied with the thief climbed up and quickly removed the eggs without the bird's noticing anything amiss.

Humans pretend that they are monkeys and climb trees. Which is all right, because humans used to be monkeys, they say. But this is not tree-climbing practice. That boy is sneaking up on a pigeon's nest. It says: "He is going to steal an egg again." Then the circus magician will put the egg in his pocket and pretend to hatch it there. It always looks as if the pigeon hatched in his pocket, but really the pigeon was hiding there all the time.

The pigeon is well trained, so that whenever the magician says, "Come out!" out it flies. When it does what it's told, it gets a tasty morsel of sugar. And if it flies off course and gets hurt, the magician will take it to the doctor. Circus animals don't have to look for their own food, and sometimes they'll be up on a stage getting lots of applause. But on the other hand, they're not free. You wouldn't like to be a circus fox, would you, Freddy?

Next, the father took the five eggs and arranged them on a table. Then he asked his third son to shoot all the eggs exactly in half with just one shot. It looked impossible, but the son took his gun, aimed carefully, and—BANG!—did just what his father had demanded.

Oh-oh! That man's got a rifle! Now, Freddy, look at this carefully. The thing that human has looks just like a stick. But it's not! A rifle is not the same as a stick at all. A thing called a bullet comes flying out of a rifle at tremendous speed. And that's no magic trick—it's real! Freddy, if you should ever run into a human being with a real rifle, get away fast. Take a good look at this picture. *That* is a rifle.

Here we have a circus magician training his rabbit and pigeon to come out at the sound of a rifle shot. But it's only the sound—there's no bullet in his gun, so there's nothing to worry about here. He's not a real hunter. He's not even very good at shooting, and besides, he wouldn't want to kill his circus animals. Actually, this is a trick table. The pigeon and a rabbit are hidden inside, and they fly out when they hear the BANG!

Then the father turned to the fourth son and asked him to sew the eggs back together again in such a way that the little chicks inside would not be harmed. The boy took out his special needle and neatly sewed the chicks and then the eggs together. This done, the first son had to climb up into the tree again and return the eggs to the nest without the mother bird's noticing anything. She continued to sit on the eggs and keep them warm, and after a few days they hatched. Each little chick came forth with only the faintest red seam to show where it had been stitched together.

See, the magician is just taking the pigeon out of his pocket. What? You say it's an egg, not a pigeon? Well, of course. Everything comes in its proper order. First he takes out the egg, then he's going to pretend to take the pigeon out of the egg. Can't you just imagine how happy that pigeon will be to be free, heading home to its nest?

Well, anyway, this is what was left after the pigeon flew off. The egg is empty. What? There's nothing strange or magical, you say, about a pigeon flying out of a pigeon egg? Well, yes, but it wasn't a baby pigeon. It flew off right away. Look, there it is in the tree. And all the people are trying to figure out what happened with the egg.

The father was very pleased to see how well the brothers had learned their trades. He could not decide which one had done the best, but before he could think of any more ways to test their skills, the village crier came riding through the town with an important announcement. Something terrible had happened, he said. A dragon had carried away the royal princess. The king and queen were very upset and promised that whoever could rescue the princess and bring her back should have her for his bride.

A trumpet sounds. But it's not a hunter's horn. It's a peaceful sound. The two people on horseback have unfurled a scroll and are letting everyone read it. The scroll says: "It is announced far and wide: The circus is here. Come one, come all!" Word spreads, and soon the circus is the talk of the town.

The king, too, heard that the circus had come. The king loved circuses. He wanted more than anything to go. What? Somebody's crying, you say? Yes, that's the queen. She is very kind-hearted and is against circuses and zoos. You see, she is against people doing what *they* want with the animals, instead of what the animals want.

"We'll rescue the princess," declared the brothers.

"First, let me find out quickly where she is," said the stargazer, as he took out his telescope and peered through it. "I see her now! She's on a big rock in the ocean, with the dragon beside her. He's watching her so she can't escape."

The brothers ran to tell this to the king, who gave them a boat. In it they rowed far out in the ocean to the rock where the poor princess was sitting. The dragon had fallen asleep with his head in her lap.

"I can't shoot him," said the hunter, "for I might hurt her, too."

"Then I'll try my skill," said the one who had studied with the thief. He climbed up the rock and carried the princess down. He did this so cleverly that the dragon never noticed a thing, and went right on snoring.

Now the circus has begun. First the wild-animal trainer comes on. Wild animals like lions and tigers are scary animals that are stronger than humans. In the old days, circuses always used lions and tigers and bears. But this circus doesn't. It has dragons and monsters, because they're even more scary. Just take their size, for instance. Look at that one. It's fifty times bigger than an elephant, and ten times bigger than a whale.

"Now presenting the Dance of the Monster," says the ringmaster. That girl has lulled the monster to sleep with a song. Even a terrible monster can be calmed down with sweet music. You don't have to hit it. Modern animal trainers don't go around cracking whips. But what will happen when this monster dances? The sea will go wild and the land will shake. It will really be something to see.

Hastily the brothers set off across the sea with the princess. But before they had gone far, the dragon awoke. When he saw that the brothers had taken the princess away from him, he was furious. He flew after them, breathing flames and roaring horribly. But as he hovered over the boat, getting ready to attack, the hunter aimed his gun and fired. BANG! The bullet hit the monster right in the heart. Down crashed the wicked dragon. . .

Oh-oh! The monster is angry! Dancing would have been bad enough, but an angry monster? Oh, dear! Human beings have pushed animals around for too long. Here it is, still sleepy, being ordered to dance! Who wouldn't get angry? Oh-oh! This is bad! There's no telling what will happen now. An angry monster is like a storm and an earthquake coming at you all at once. Even a wild animal trainer could never handle this.

Oh dear! Oh dear! What's to be done? Don't ask me. The only thing left is to call out the army. Maybe that's the army in the boat there. They've got rifles. Hey, fire is shooting out of the rifles! And there goes the first shot: BANG! A little gun like that isn't going to help. The monster will just get angrier than ever. It'll start a storm and the circus tent will blow away. Oh, this is just what I was afraid of!

. . . right on top of the boat! It was so terribly big and heavy it broke the boat into a thousand pieces. It was a catastrophe!

What did I tell you? Oh, dear! The circus is a mess. They should have stopped with the rifle. Now it looks like they've hauled out a cannon. The monster has either been blasted to smithereens or it's dived into the sea. There has definitely been a calamity here. Look. The boats and people have all been blown away. I hope this is the end of it, but I'm afraid other monsters will come to help this one. That's why I always say: Never tease animals.

I knew something like this would happen. The circus would have been scary enough. But with the mountains and seas all in turmoil like this, I wouldn't be surprised if all of the mountains became volcanoes and erupted, just like when the earth was born. The forests and fields, the towns and villages—they'll all be blasted away. Oh, it's frightening. Freddy, hang on tight to Father's hand. I'll protect you, come what may.

But the fourth brother, who had studied with the tailor, took out his magic needle and quickly stitched the pieces of the boat together again. He even made a sail from the dragon's skin, and soon they were all on their way home.

Hey, what's this? The storm is over. Just when I thought the world had gone topsy-turvy, everything calms down. This is some circus! The monster seems to have turned into a boat. They get the audience all worked up into thinking that it's the end of the world, then suddenly stop the storm and return everything back to the way it was. Wow! This is some circus! Foxes can turn themselves into a lot of things, but a *boat…?* Incredible!

Just listen to that clapping! The audience is thrilled. Can you hear the sound of that applause? Isn't that something? Let's hope all this clapping noise doesn't bring on another storm. The sea is a bit rough, but it's gradually calming down. A nice breeze has begun to blow, and the sail is billowing out. And that girl is back in the boat. The storm warning has been lifted. And so everything ended well with the circus.

The king and queen were overjoyed when they saw their daughter again.

"One of you shall have my daughter for his bride," said the king. "You will have to decide amongst yourselves which one it will be. You are all heroes."

But now, sad to say, the brothers began to quarrel and shout at each other. Each one of them felt that if it were not for his particular skill the princess would not have been saved.

Thank goodness! What a relief! The king, who was watching the circus, is happy, too. The circus was so good that the king invited the entire troupe back to his castle. He held a big party for them. What's that? You think that girl looks like the one who put the monster to sleep? You're right, Freddy. And there is an interesting story about her.

This girl is very pretty and smart. And since the king didn't have any children, he asked her if she wouldn't come and be the princess in his castle. It says in the book that the queen asked her to come, too. This was wonderful. After all, you can't have a castle without a princess. And, besides, once she became a princess, she wouldn't allow any fox hunting.

Leaving the girl—I mean the princess—behind, the circus troupe set off again. Without the girl, there would be no more "Transformation of the Monster" act, but that couldn't be helped. In what town square will the circus open tomorrow? There is something sad about the ending. Yes, it's always sad when a circus is over. And not only a circus, Freddy, it's always sad when something fun is over.

Finally, the king declared, "Each of you has an equal right to marry the princess, but since you cannot all have her, then none of you shall have her. Instead, as your reward for saving her life, I will make all of you princes and give each of you an equal portion of my kingdom."

So it was that all of the four clever brothers became wealthy princes. They went back home cheerfully and lived with their father in great happiness for many a long year.

"Again! Read it again, Daddy," begged little Freddy Fox. "No, Freddy. You know I told you I could only read it once," said Mr. Fox, settling back in his chair and taking off his spectacles. "It's time for my nap. And you mustn't ask anyone else to read these stories to you, Freddy. We promised, remember?" Freddy couldn't understand why in the world his father wouldn't read the book again. Can you guess the reason?

About the Brothers Grimm

Wilhelm Grimm (1789–1859) and his brother Jakob (1785–1863) were German scholars and linguists who worked harmoniously as a team throughout their lives. The wonderful folk and fairy stories associated with their names were not invented by them, but were collected from the oral tradition of the common people near their home in Hesse. Published in several volumes from 1812 to 1824 as *Kinder- und Hausmärchen,* they were an immediate success and were soon translated into English and other languages. After the restraints of eighteenth-century classicism, the Romantic movement was just beginning, and the Grimms' stories of princesses and shepherds, of talking animals, of witches, magicians, and astrologers found a ready audience among adults as well as children.

About Mitsumasa Anno

Mitsumasa Anno is known around the world for his beautiful and imaginative picture books, for which he has received the Hans Christian Andersen Award and many other honors. Born in Tsuwano, a small historic town in western Japan, he now lives in Tokyo, but he travels a great deal, with sketchbook and camera always at hand. After graduating from Yamaguchi Teacher Training College, Mr. Anno taught art at a school in Tokyo before deciding to devote himself entirely to writing and illustrating. All of his many books reflect his innovative approach to teaching, as well as his belief in the ability of children to make their own learning discoveries. Mr. Anno believes in encouraging children to stretch their imaginations, to look beneath the surface appearances of things. His approach is humorous and entertaining, for he feels that learning should be a joyful experience.

About Mr. Fox he says, "It is a little poignant that he has to conceal the fact that he can't read. It is a joke I share with the reader of the stories, but it is also a little sad. He loves his son Freddy, and of course he wants Freddy to look up to him and admire him. In his position, I think I might do the same thing. In fact, you might say that Mr. Fox and I are quite a lot alike!"

The range of Mitsumasa Anno's works includes mathematics (*Anno's Math Games I, II* and *III; Anno's Counting House, Anno's Mysterious Multiplying Jar*), history (*Anno's Medieval World*), geography and social studies (*Anno's USA, Anno's Britain, Anno's Journey*), logic (*Anno's Hat Tricks, Socrates and the Three Little Pigs*), nature (*Anno's Animals*), art (*Anno's Magical ABC, The Unique World of Mitsumasa Anno*), science (*All in a Day, Anno's Sundial*) and world literature and folklore (*Anno's Aesop, Anno's Twice Told Tales*), to name just a few.

The illustrations for this book were executed in watercolor and pencil.
The publishers wish to thank Jean Inglis and Eva L. Mayer for their valuable assistance with
the translation of some parts of this book from the Japanese and the German, respectively.
The source for the Grimms' stories here is *Kinder- und Hausmärchen,* collected by Jakob and
Wilhelm Grimm. Mr. Fox's stories, of course, are all original tales by Mitsumasa Anno.

First published in Japanese in 1991 by Iwanami Shoten, Publishers, Tokyo.
First American edition published in 1993 by Philomel Books, a division of
the Putnam & Grosset Group, 200 Madison Avenue, New York, NY 10016.
Published simultaneously in Canada. Printed in Hong Kong.
Book design by Colleen Flis. The text of Grimm's tales is set in 11 point Caslon 540;
the text of Mr. Fox's stories is set in 13 point Caslon Old Face.
Library of Congress Cataloging-in-Publication Data
Anno, Mitsumasa, 1926–   [Kitsune ga hirotta Gurimu dōwa. English] Anno's twice told tales:
The fisherman and his wife & The four clever brothers / by the Brothers Grimm & Mr. Fox;
[retold and] illustrated by Mitsumasa Anno.   p.   cm.
Summary: Presents two tales from the Brothers Grimm, combined with Mr. Fox's highly
unusual interpretations of them. 1. Fairy tales—Germany. [1. Fairy tales. 2. Folklore—
Germany.] I. Grimm, Jacob, 1785–1863. II. Grimm, Wilhelm,
1786–1859. III. Title. PZ7.A59An 1993 398.22—dc20 [E]92-25307 CIP AC
ISBN 0-399-22005-4
1 3 5 7 9 8 6 4 2
First American Edition